Walt Disney's

PETER PAN
and
WENDY

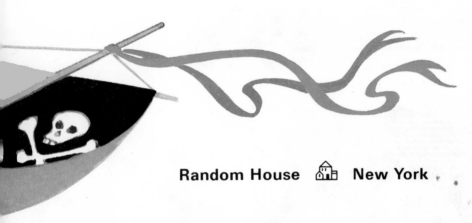

Random House  **New York**

Book Club Edition

First American Edition. Copyright © 1981 by The Walt Disney Company. All rights reserved under International and Pan-American Copyright Conventions. Published in the United States by Random House, Inc., New York, and simultaneously in Canada by Random House of Canada Limited, Toronto. Originally published in Denmark as PETER PAN OG WENDY by Gutenberghus Gruppen, Copenhagen. ISBN: 0-394-84973-6 Manufactured in the United States of America
9 10   L M N O P

The Darling family lived on a quiet street
in London.

There were three children in the family—
Wendy, John, and little Michael.

The children had a nurse called Nana.

Nana was a Saint Bernard dog.

Nana was a good nurse.
She walked the children to school
in the morning.

And she picked them up in the afternoon.

Nana made sure that the children ate
their spinach at dinner.

And all night she stayed by their beds.

At bedtime Wendy always told stories
to her brothers.

Her best story was about Peter Pan.

"Peter Pan lives in Neverland," she
told them. "It is a magic place where
children never grow up. There are
fairies in Neverland, and wild animals,
and pirates, too!"

One night Mother and Father came in
to say good night before a party.

They found the boys in the middle of
a noisy pirate fight.

"Stop it at once!" said Father. "You
are too old to play pirates. And you are
too old to have a nurse, too!"

Father put Nana on a leash.

"Wendy," he said, "you look after your brothers. And no more stories!"

Father took Nana downstairs and tied her up in the yard.

Then he and Mother went off to the party.

Poor Nana!
She was unhappy away from the children.

Then in through the bedroom window flew
Peter Pan and the fairy Tinker Bell!
Peter loved Wendy's stories.
He hid outside the window every night
and listened to them.

Peter had heard what Father said.

"Come to Neverland with me!" said Peter. "Wendy can tell stories to me and my friends, the Lost Boys. John and Michael can help me fight pirates!"

"Hooray!" said John.

"How will we get to Neverland?" asked
Wendy.

"We will fly!" said Peter.
He threw some fairy dust on the children.

"Now, think happy
thoughts!" said Peter.
So the children did.
In a twinkling, they all
floated up to the ceiling.
"We're flying!" they cried.

Out the window the children flew.

"Follow me!" called Peter Pan. "This way
to Neverland!"

Down in the yard, Nana barked and barked.
But no one heard her.

Peter and the children flew and flew.
Finally they reached Neverland.
They landed safely on a cloud.
But right below them were pirates—
Captain Hook and his mate, Mr. Smee!

Captain Hook hated Peter Pan.

He was always trying to capture Peter.

He looked up and saw Peter on the cloud.

"Now I've got you!" shouted Captain Hook.

"Mr. Smee, fire the cannon!"

The cannonball whizzed
through the air.
It just missed Peter and
the children!
"Whew! That was close!"
said John.

"It is too dangerous here,"
said Peter. "Tink, you take
the children to the Lost Boys.
I will stay and keep an eye
on Hook."

John and Michael wanted
to watch the pirates, too.
But Peter made them go
with Tinker Bell.

The children followed Tink to the home
of Peter and the Lost Boys.
They lived in a secret cave under
an old tree.

The Lost Boys did not have a mother.
So they were very happy to see Wendy.
When Peter got to the cave, he said,
"Three cheers for Wendy, boys! She is
going to tell us stories."

"Hooray! Hooray! Hooray!" cried the boys.
But Tinker Bell did not say hooray.
Tink felt left out.
She tried to think of something mean
to do to Wendy.
She decided to go see Captain Hook!

Tinker Bell told
Captain Hook all
about Wendy.

"I can help you get rid of Wendy," said
Captain Hook. "I will capture her and make
her scrub the decks of my ship!"

Tinker Bell looked pleased.

"There is just one thing," said Hook
with a wicked smile. "I do not know where
to find Wendy. You must show me where
Peter lives."

So Tink marked a path to the secret cave
on Captain Hook's map.

She did not guess that the pirate planned
to capture Peter!

At the cave, Wendy was telling stories.

Peter and the Lost Boys wanted to hear every story she knew.

But John and Michael began to miss Mother and Father.

Finally Wendy said, "It is time to go home."
"I don't want you to leave!" cried Peter.
He would not even say good-bye.
Waving sadly, Wendy followed her brothers
and the Lost Boys out of the cave.

Tinker Bell
was happy to
see Wendy go!

Outside the cave, the pirate crew was waiting!

The men captured the children as they came out of the cave.

Wendy and the boys were marched off to Captain Hook.

"Blast you, Smee!" said Hook when he saw the children. "You did not bring me Peter Pan!"

Tinker Bell heard Captain Hook.
Now she knew that Hook had tricked her!
He only wanted to capture Peter Pan.
Tink flew to tell Peter what had happened.
Maybe Peter could save the children.

The pirates took the children to the ship.

Captain Hook said to the children, "You can all join up with me and be pirates—or you can walk the plank!"

Wendy was not afraid of Captain Hook.

"I will NEVER be a pirate!" she cried.

"Then you will be the first to walk the plank," said Hook.

He tied Wendy's hands behind her back.

Wendy bravely started
to walk the plank.
All of a sudden, Peter
and Tinker Bell flew onto
the pirate ship!

Peter and Tink quickly cut the ropes
around the children.

Then Peter and the children
began to chase the pirates.

Peter flew everywhere with
his sword.

What a fight there was!

Most of the pirates jumped off
the ship.

Wendy and the boys cheered.

The last pirate left
was Captain Hook.
Peter flew around
and around him.
Captain Hook tried
to catch Peter.

But Peter was too fast for Captain Hook.
Hook got dizzy and fell into the sea—
right beside a hungry crocodile!

Captain Hook swam for his life!

"Ha, ha, ha!" called Peter.

Then Peter threw some fairy dust
on the children.

And away they all flew.

Peter flew back to London with Wendy,
John, and Michael.

He left them at their bedroom window.

"Good-bye, Peter!" cried the children.

The next morning, Father let Nana
come back in the house.
The children were happy to see her.
And they were happy to be home again.

But they never forgot their trip
to Neverland.